About this book

This book is for everyone who is learning their first words in Spanish. By looking at the little pictures, it will be easy to read and remember the Spanish words underneath.

When you look at the Spanish words, you will see that in front of most of them, there is **la** or **el**, which means "the". When you are learning Spanish, it is a good idea to learn the **la** or **el** which goes with each one. This is because all words, like *book* and *table*, as well as *boy* and *girl*, are masculine or feminine. **La** means the word is feminine and **el** usually means that it is masculine. If the word is plural, that is, there is more than one, such as *tables* or *books*, then it has **las** or **los** in front of it. **Las** is the feminine and **los** is the masculine.

Some of the words have an n with a squiggle over it, like this **ñ**. The squiggle is called a tilde. In Spanish this **ñ** is a separate letter in the alphabet and is said differently from the ordinary **n**. Some letters have accents on them. This does not change the sound of the letter but changes the way the word is said.

At the back of the book is a guide to help you say all the words in the pictures. But there are some sounds in Spanish which are quite different from any sound in English. To say a Spanish word correctly, you really need to hear a Spanish speaker say it first. Listen very carefully and then try to say it that way yourself. But if you say a word as it is written in the guide, a Spanish person will understand you, even if your Spanish accent is not perfect.

Usborne
First
hundred
words
in Spanish

Heather Amery
Illustrated by Stephen Cartwright

Translation and Pronunciation Guide by Jane Straker
American editor: Carrie A. Seay
Designed by Mike Olley and Jan McCafferty

 There is a little yellow duck to find in every picture.

En la sala
In the living room

el papá
Daddy

la mamá
Mommy

el niño
boy

2

la niña
girl

el bebé
baby

el perro
dog

el gato
cat

3

Vestirse Getting dressed

los zapatos
shoes

los calzones
underwear

el suéter
sweater

4

la camiseta
undershirt

el pantalón
pants

la camiseta
t-shirt

los calcetines
socks

5

En la cocina In the kitchen

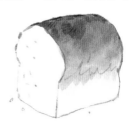

el pan
bread

la leche
milk

los huevos
eggs

la manzana
apple

la naranja
orange

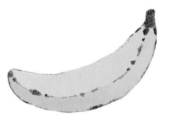

el plátano
banana

Lavar los platos

Cleaning up

la mesa
table

la silla
chair

el plato
plate

8

el cuchillo
knife

el tenedor
fork

la cuchara
spoon

la taza
cup

La hora del juego <small>Play time</small>

el caballo
horse

la oveja
sheep

la vaca
cow

la gallina
hen

el cerdo
pig

el tren
train

los cubos
blocks

De visita   Going on a visit

la abuela
Grandma

el abuelo
Grandpa

las zapatillas
slippers

12

el abrigo
coat

el vestido
dress

el gorro
hat

En el parque In the park

el árbol
tree

la flor
flower

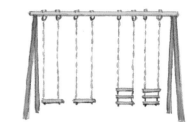

los columpios
swings

el balón
ball

el tobogán
slide

las botas
boots

el pájaro
bird

el barco
boat

Por la calle In the street

el coche
car

la bicicleta
bicycle

el avión
airplane

la camioneta
truck

el autobús
bus

la casa
house

Celebrar una fiesta Having a party

el globo
balloon

el pastel
cake

el reloj
clock

el helado
ice cream

el pez
fish

las galletas
cookies

los caramelos
candy

19

Nadar Swimming

el brazo
arm

la mano
hand

la pierna
leg

los pies
feet

los dedos
de los pies
toes

la cabeza
head

el trasero
bottom

21

En el vestuario

In the changing room

la boca

mouth

los ojos

eyes

las orejas

ears

la nariz
nose

el pelo
hair

el peine
comb

el cepillo
brush

23

Ir de compras

rojo
red

azul
blue

verde
green

amarillo
yellow

rosa
pink

blanco
white

negro
black

En el cuarto de baño In the bathroom

el jabón
soap

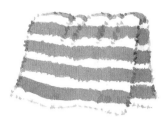

la toalla
towel

el wáter
toilet

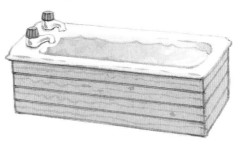

la bañera
bathtub

la barriguita
tummy

el pato
duck

En el dormitorio

In the bedroom

la cama
bed

la lámpara
light

la ventana
window

28

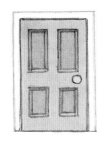

la puerta
door

el libro
book

la muñeca
doll

el osito
teddy bear

29

Match the words to the pictures

el balón

las botas

los calcetines

la camiseta

el cerdo

el coche

el cuchillo

el gato

el gorro

el helado

el huevo

la lámpara

la leche

el libro

la manzana

la mesa

la muñeca

la naranja

el osito

el pastel

el pato

el perro

el pez

el plátano

el reloj

el suéter

el tenedor

el tren

la vaca

la ventana

Contar   Counting

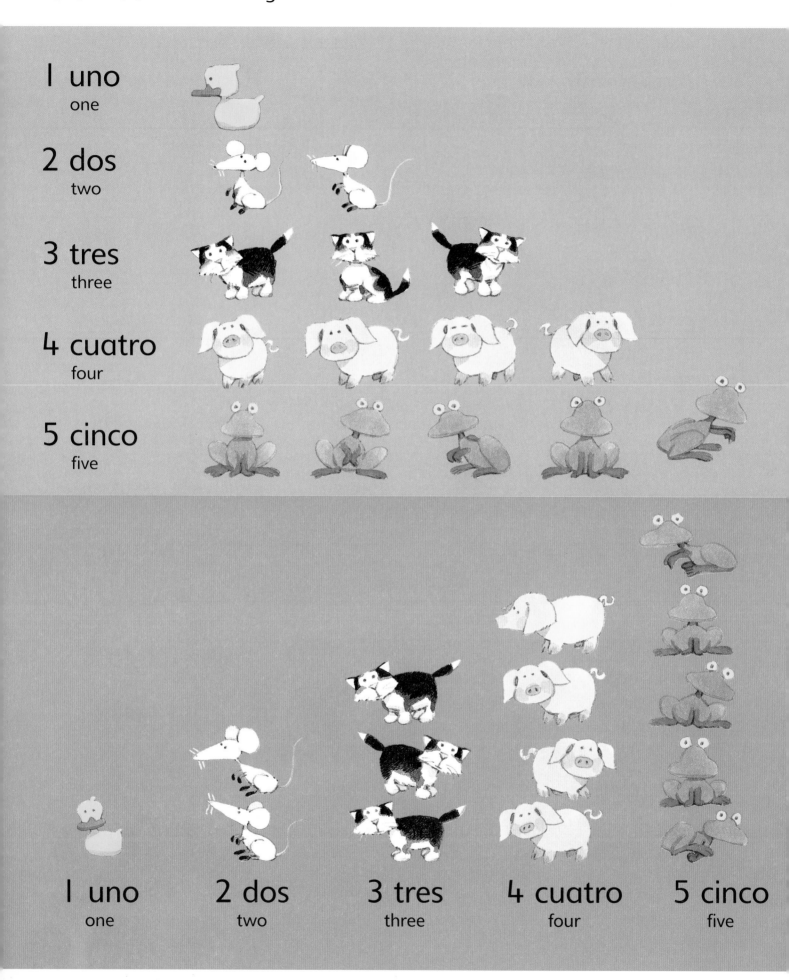

1 uno
one

2 dos
two

3 tres
three

4 cuatro
four

5 cinco
five

1 uno
one

2 dos
two

3 tres
three

4 cuatro
four

5 cinco
five

Words in the pictures

In this alphabetical list of all the words in the pictures, the Spanish word comes first, next is the guide to saying the word, and then there is the English translation. The guide may look strange or funny, but just try to read it as if it were English words. It will help you to say the words in Spanish correctly, if you remember these rules:

Capital, or BIG, letters show which part of the word to stress:

a   is said like **a** in h**a**ppen

e   is said like **e** in h**e**lp

o   is said like **o** in h**o**rse

ch is quite different from any sound in the English language but it is said like the **ch** in the Scottish word lo**ch**

rrr is **r** rolled on your tongue, like the **r** in the name of the Scottish poet Bu**r**ns

abrigo	*aBREEgo*	coat	celebrar	*sseleBRAR*	celebrate
abuela	*aBWEla*	Grandma	cepillo	*ssePEELyo*	brush
abuelo	*aBWElo*	Grandpa	cerdo	*SSERdo*	pig
amarillo	*amaREELyo*	yellow	cinco	*SSEENko*	five
árbol	*ARbol*	tree	coche	*KOTshe*	car
autobús	*aootoBOOSS*	bus	cocina	*koSSEEna*	kitchen
avión	*abeeONN*	airplane	columpios	*koLOOMpyoss*	swings
azul	*aSSOOL*	blue	compras	*KOMprass*	shopping
			contar	*konTAR*	counting
balón	*baLONN*	ball	cuarto de baño	*kwartodeBANyo*	bathroom
bañera	*baNYEra*	bathtub	cuatro	*KWAtro*	four
barco	*BARko*	boat	cubos	*KOOboss*	blocks
barriguita	*barrreeGEEta*	tummy	cuchara	*kootSHAra*	spoon
bebé	*beBE*	baby	cuchillo	*kootSHEELyo*	knife
bicicleta	*beesseeKLEta*	bicycle			
blanco	*BLANko*	white	dedos	*dedoss-*	toes
boca	*BOka*	mouth	de los pies	*delossPYESS*	
botas	*BOtass*	boots	dormitorio	*dormeeTORyo*	bedroom
brazo	*BRAsso*	arm	dos	*doss*	two
caballo	*kaBALyo*	horse	fiesta	*FYESSta*	party
cabeza	*kaBEssa*	head	flor	*flor*	flower
calcetines	*kalsseTEEness*	socks			
calle	*KALye*	street	galletas	*galYEtass*	cookies
calzones	*kalSSOness*	underwear	gallina	*galYEEna*	hen
cama	*KAma*	bed	gato	*GAto*	cat
camioneta	*kameeoNEta*	truck	globo	*GLObo*	balloon
camiseta	*kameeSSEta*	undershirt, t-shirt	gorro	*GOrrro*	hat
caramelos	*karaMEloss*	candy	helado	*eLAdo*	ice cream
casa	*KAssa*	house	hora	*Ora*	time

Spanish	Pronunciation	English
huevos	WEboss	eggs
jabón	chaBONN	soap
juego	CHWEgo	game
lámpara	LAMpara	light
lavar	laBAR	clean
leche	LETshe	milk
libro	LEEbro	book
mamá	maMA	Mommy
mano	MAno	hand
manzana	manSSAna	apple
mesa	MEssa	table
muñeca	mooNYEka	doll
nadar	naDAR	swimming
naranja	naRANcha	orange
nariz	naREESS	nose
negro	NEgro	black
niña	NEENya	girl
niño	NEENyo	boy
ojos	ochos	eyes
orejas	oREchas	ears
osito	oSEEto	teddy bear
oveja	oBEcha	sheep
pájaro	PAcharo	bird
pan	pann	bread
pantalón	pantaLONN	pants
papá	paPA	Daddy
parque	PARke	park
pastel	passTEL	cake
pato	PAto	duck
peine	PEYne	comb
pelo	PElo	hair
perro	PErrro	dog
pez	pess	fish
pierna	PYERna	leg
pies	pyess	feet
plátano	PLAtano	banana
plato	PLAto	plate
puerta	PWERta	door
reloj	rrreLOCH	clock
rojo	RRROcho	red
rosa	ROssa	pink
sala	SSAla	living room
silla	SSEELya	chair
suéter	SSWEter	sweater
taza	TAssa	cup
tenedor	teneDOR	fork
toalla	toALya	towel
tobogán	toboGANN	slide
trasero	trassERo	bottom
tren	trenn	train
tres	tress	three
uno	OOno	one
vaca	BAka	cow
ventana	benTAna	window
verde	BERde	green
vestido	besTEEdo	dress
vestirse	besTEERse	getting dressed
vestuario	bestooAReeo	changing room
visita	beeSEEta	visit
wáter	WAter	toilet
zapatillas	ssapaTEELyas	slippers
zapatos	ssaPAtoss	shoes

This edition first published in 2002 by Usborne Publishing Ltd, Usborne House, 83-85 Saffron Hill, London EC1N 8RT, England.
www.usborne.com
Copyright © 2002, 1991, 1988 Usborne Publishing Ltd. This edition first published in America 2002. AE.